NFL TODAY

KANSAS CITY CHIEFS

LOREN STANLEY

CREATIVE EDUCATION

Published by Creative Education
123 South Broad Street, Mankato, Minnesota 56001
Creative Education is an imprint of The Creative Company

Designed by Rita Marshall
Cover illustration by Rob Day

Photos by: Allsport Photography, Associated Press, Bettmann Archive,
Focus on Sports, Fotosport, Spectra Action, and SportsChrome.

Copyright © 1997 Creative Education.
International copyrights reserved in all countries.
No part of this book may be reproduced in any form without written
permission from the publisher.
Printed in the United States of America.

Library of Congress Cataloging-in-Publication Data

Stanley, Loren, 1951-
Kansas City Chiefs / by Loren Stanley.
p. cm. — (NFL Today)
Summary: Traces the history of the team from its beginnings through 1996.
ISBN 0-88682-813-9

1. Kansas City Chiefs (Football team)—History—Juvenile literature.
[1. Kansas City Chiefs (Football team) 2. Football—History.]
I. Title. II. Series.

GV956.K35S83 1996   96-15244
796.332'64'09778411—dc20

123456

Kansas City is the second-largest city in the state of Missouri. Kansas City is also the second-largest city in the state of Kansas. Confused? It's simple, although sometimes it doesn't seem that way. There are two Kansas Cities, and they are right next to each other. The Kansas City in Missouri is located at the western edge of the state. The Kansas City in Kansas is at the eastern edge of that state. They are both located on the Missouri River.

Kansas City, Missouri, is a city of almost 450,000 citizens, which makes it almost three times as big as the other Kansas City. Kansas City, Missouri, is also home to the only pro football

All-time Kansas City great, Len Dawson.

The Chiefs were originally known as the Dallas Texans.

team based in either Missouri or Kansas—the Kansas City Chiefs.

The Chiefs didn't start out in Kansas City, though. The team began play in 1960 and was known as the Dallas Texans. When the American Football League was formed in 1960, the Texans were one of the original eight teams. Their owner, Lamar Hunt, was a Texan, and he wanted his team to play in his home state. But Hunt had a problem. The same year the AFL began play, the older, more established National Football League put an expansion team known as the Cowboys in Dallas. The NFL wasn't about to let the AFL have Dallas without a fight. As it turned out, it would be a losing battle for Hunt and the AFL.

Dawson Passes the Test in the AFL

While Hunt looked for another city in which to settle his team, the Texans and their coach, Hank Stram, prepared to play the 1962 season. In training camp that year was a new quarterback who had played five years in the NFL. Lenny Dawson had been with the Pittsburgh Steelers and the Cleveland Browns, and he was considered a good player with a lot of potential. But both Cleveland and Pittsburgh decided to let him go. They would regret that decision.

Stram had been an assistant at Purdue University when Dawson played there. But Dawson wasn't the same quarterback Stram had seen at Purdue and in the NFL. One day, Stram went over to talk to his new quarterback.

"I never realized how many bad habits you've developed," Stram told Dawson. "You have your work cut out for you. I know you can do the job, but we'll have to reach back and put it all together again."

In the '80s, Bill Kenney struggled to replace Dawson (page 7).

TD Man! The club record for the most touchdowns in a season was set by running back Abner Haynes with 19.

Stram had given him a wake-up call. Later that day, Dawson spoke to Stram. "Believe me, Hank, I had no idea that I've gotten so out of the groove," Dawson said. "The trouble is, nobody ever worked with me or talked to me about technique or execution during the five years I spent in the NFL. However, I'm ready to buckle down and work under your direction."

Stram was impressed with Dawson's reaction. The coach had sent his message and it had been received. Led by Dawson, the Texans rolled to an 11-3 record and won the Western Division of the AFL. Helping Dawson and Stram was halfback Abner Haynes, who scored 19 touchdowns to set a league record.

In the 1962 league championship game, Dallas beat its Texas rivals, the Houston Oilers, 20-17 in sudden-death overtime. Dawson was named AFL Player of the Year. Yet despite the success, the Dallas fans did not support the team. Attendance at games was disappointing. As a result, after the season, the Texans moved to Kansas City and became the Chiefs.

The change of scenery also changed the team's luck. The Texans had finished as winners. The Chiefs didn't start out that way. Kansas City wound up third in the Western Division in 1963 with a 5-7-2 record. But the team, with Dawson at quarterback, battled back.

CHIEFS RECEIVE A GIFT IN OTIS TAYLOR

The Chiefs improved, but they still hadn't returned to championship status. They needed more weapons; in 1965 the Chiefs found one. They drafted a wide receiver with a world of talent. Kansas City scout Lloyd Wills couldn't believe how good Otis Taylor was. "I thought when I first saw him and still think now that for pure natural ability, there has never been anyone like Otis," Wills commented. "He can do what he wants to do. When I go out now and look at wide receivers, I compare them to Otis."

What made Taylor special was his size and strength. He was huge by wide receiver standards, 6-foot-3 and 215 pounds. "Some receivers have great speed and great moves," Dawson said. "Otis has both plus size and strength."

Taylor knew exactly how good he was. He demanded a lot from himself and was never satisfied with anything less than excellence. "I'll tell you something about Otis Taylor," Taylor said. "He wants to be the best—always. There hasn't been a year when he didn't want to score more touchdowns than anybody and gain more yardage than anybody. At the start of the season, I aim for the top ten and higher. And I don't quit."

Stolen! Super thief Emmitt Thomas intercepted twelve passes during the season.

The Chiefs didn't quit in 1966 until they had won the Western Division and then defeated the Buffalo Bills in the league championship game. In past years the season ended after the AFL title game. Not in 1966. The AFL champion Chiefs played the NFL champs, the Green Bay Packers. The game was called the AFL-NFL Championship Game. Lamar Hunt didn't like that name. "Why don't we just call it the Super Bowl," Hunt suggested. That name would stick.

The Chiefs weren't given much of a chance to defeat the powerful Packers. But the fans were obviously curious to see how the game would come out. More than 65 million people watched the game on television, the largest single audience for an athletic event in the history of television.

What the viewers saw was the Chiefs matching Green Bay's early score with one of their own, tying the game 7-7 in the

The Chiefs stretched for greatness in the 1960s (pages 10-11).

Wide receiver Otis Taylor caught 59 passes for 958 yards and 11 touchdowns.

second quarter on Dawson's seven-yard pass to fullback Curtis McClinton. Kansas City closely trailed 14-10 at halftime, but the Chiefs ran out of gas in the second half. Behind quarterback Bart Starr, the Packers ran away to a 35-10 victory. Green Bay managed to shut down Kansas City's offense in the second half.

All the experts had expected the Chiefs to lose. After all, they said, the older NFL was clearly a better league than the younger AFL. Those experts would soon be singing a different tune. In 1968 the New York Jets shocked the football world. The Jets, champs of the AFL, defeated NFL champion Baltimore 16-7 in Super Bowl III. The experts weren't impressed. A fluke, they called it. Wait till next year, they said. Next year was 1969, and the AFL champ was Kansas City.

The Chiefs now became the first AFL team to play in two Super Bowls. The opponent this time was the Minnesota Vikings. The odds makers said the Vikings were 13-point favorites, but the Chiefs weren't impressed. This was a different Kansas City team than the one that lost in Super Bowl I. Said Dawson, "I got a great indication of the feeling of the players when one of my linemen came up to me and said, 'Don't worry about it. We can beat these guys.'"

But Dawson had other worries. A couple of days before the Super Bowl, a report surfaced that linked Dawson to professional gamblers. The Kansas City quarterback was accused of betting on pro football games, including those played by the Chiefs. If true, such charges could lead to a lifetime ban from football. But these charges had no factual basis. Still, the rumors bothered Dawson. They angered his teammates as well. The Chiefs were now even more ready than ever.

Kansas City dominated the Vikings in the first half. Dawson

directed the team on three long drives, but the Chiefs could not get the ball in the end zone. They had to settle for three Jan Stenerud field goals. Late in the half, Dawson drove Kansas City to the Vikings' 5-yard line. On third down, Minnesota's defenders braced for an expected pass. Dawson rolled out to his right, but then handed the ball to Mike Garrett, who ran back to the left and into the end zone. The Vikings were stunned. They also were behind 16-0.

In the second half, the Vikings scored a touchdown early in the third quarter. It appeared the momentum had swung Minnesota's way. But Dawson and the Chiefs responded to the challenge. From the Vikings 46-yard line, Dawson faded back and threw a sideline pass to Taylor. Although it was a play designed to get a first down and not much more, Taylor had other ideas. "It was only a 6-yard pass," he said. "I got hit on the left side and spun out. Then I hit the last guy downfield with my hand. I always try to punish a pass defender, just as he does me. I wanted to score that touchdown."

Chiefs rookie center Jack Rudnay anchored an offensive line that protected quarterback Len Dawson.

Taylor, who broke two hard tackles before scoring, gave the Chiefs a 23-7 lead on the remarkable pass and run. Dawson knew the game was over. "That was the touchdown I wanted," Dawson said. "I knew we had them...I could sense the frustrations of the Minnesota defense. They weren't able to do the things they had been doing all year against the NFL teams."

The game ended 23-7. The scoreboard in Tulane Stadium in New Orleans said Super Chiefs in huge letters. And they had been super. They destroyed a team that was supposed to win by two touchdowns. Dawson, who was named Player of the Game, had an almost flawless contest, completing 12 of 17 passes. In the locker room afterward, reporters asked Dawson how

1 9 7 1

Placekicker Jan Stenerud enjoyed a banner year, accounting for 100 points, including 26 field goals.

the Chiefs had been able to move the ball consistently against the best defense in football. "Our game plan really wasn't very complicated," Dawson said. "It involved throwing a lot of formations at them—formations they hadn't seen during the course of the season."

The Chiefs had risen to the top of the NFL, and they had every reason to believe they would stay on top. When the NFL and AFL merged in 1970, the Chiefs were placed in the American Football Conference Western Division along with the Oakland Raiders, Denver Broncos, and San Diego Chargers. It was a strong division because both the Chiefs and Raiders had powerful teams. Oakland won the AFC West in 1970, but Kansas City took the division title in 1971. That earned the Chiefs the right to host the Miami Dolphins in the first round of the playoffs. The game was on Christmas Day, but for awhile it appeared a winner wouldn't be decided until after the New Year.

Dawson hit Elmo Wright on a 63-yard touchdown pass to give the Chiefs a 24-17 lead in the fourth quarter. Miami tied the score with 90 seconds left. Dawson then drove Kansas City into field-goal range, but the usually reliable Jan Stenerud missed the kick. The game went into sudden-death overtime, but there would not be anything sudden about the ending to this game.

Both Stenerud and Dolphins kicker Garo Yepremian had chances to kick the game winner in the fifth quarter, but both missed. The game went into the sixth quarter—only the second time in pro football history that a game had gone so long. Ironically, the only other time was 1962, when the Dallas Texans, later to become the Chiefs, defeated the Houston Oilers in the AFL championship game. This time the Chiefs would wind up losers. Yepremian got another chance midway through the sixth quarter. His field goal split the uprights, and the Dolphins won

Linebacker Willie Lanier was a stalwart force in the 1970s.

Dominant defensive end Art Still made the first of four Pro Bowl appearances.

27-24. The longest game in NFL history was finally over. To this day no NFL game has lasted any longer than the 82 minutes and 40 seconds the Chiefs and Dolphins battled.

The game was the last ever played in Kansas City's Municipal Stadium. Unfortunately for the Chiefs, the game was also the last post-season game the team would play for 15 years. The Chiefs moved to the new Arrowhead Stadium in 1972. It was a gorgeous place to play, with almost 80,000 seats—30,000 more than Municipal Stadium had. While the Chiefs kept winning in 1972 and 1973, they didn't make the playoffs. After a 5-9 season in 1974, Stram was fired. A year later both Dawson and Taylor retired. The team slid to the bottom of the AFC West in the late 1970s and stayed there for several years.

DELANEY MAKES BIG, BUT TRAGIC IMPACT

The Chiefs struggled until 1980, when new coach Marv Levy brought the team back to respectability. Kansas City finished 8-8 and expected bigger things in 1981. The addition of a rookie running back in 1981 made Kansas City one of the most improved teams in the NFL. Joe Delaney came out of Northwestern State University in Louisiana. The school was small, and so was Joe, but he was incredibly fast. In his rookie year, Delaney gained 1,121 yards, a Kansas City team record, and was named AFC Rookie of the Year.

Behind Delaney, the Chiefs nearly made the playoffs in 1981, but late-season injuries and inconsistency at quarterback doomed the team's hopes. Kansas City finished 9-7. The following year, a players' strike wiped out almost half the games. Still, Delaney had another solid season and was considered by many experts

Cornerback Albert Lewis was a Pro Bowler in the 1980s.

to be one of the best backs in the game. But on June 29, 1983, a hot day in Monroe, Louisiana, all that changed—tragically.

Joe Delaney believed in the importance of helping his fellow human beings. On this day, he noticed three young boys swimming in a lake. Delaney was on the shore of the lake playing catch with some friends. Suddenly, he heard the three boys cry for help. A little boy ran up to Delaney and said, "Can you swim?"

"I can't swim good, but I've got to save those kids," Delaney told his friends. "If I don't come up, get somebody." So Delaney, who was not much of a swimmer, jumped in the lake to try to save the three boys.

"He was scared of water any deeper than his waist," said Delaney's sister Lucille. "It was amazing that he would rush in after those boys." But Delaney did rush in, and he didn't come

1 9 8 1

AFC Rookie of the Year Joe Delaney averaged 4.8 yards per carry.

back. One of the boys managed to make it to shore. Two of the boys drowned. Joe Delaney didn't survive either. One of pro football's brightest young stars was dead at age 24.

"People ask me, 'How could Joe have gone in the water the way he did?'" said Delaney's college coach, A.L. Williams. "And I answer, 'Why, he never gave it a second thought, because helping people was a conditioned reflex to Joe Delaney.'"

On July 4, 1983, they had a funeral for Joe Delaney. All of his high school and college friends, teammates and coaches were there. So were Marv Levy and Chiefs owner Lamar Hunt. Levy gave this tribute in his eulogy: "Joe was a person who was genuine and honest right to the core of his being."

Joe Delaney was gone, and so were the team's winning ways. In 1983, the Chiefs slipped to last place in the AFC West. Levy was fired and replaced by John Mackovic, who built a winning team thanks to quarterback Bill Kenney and an excellent defense that featured perhaps the finest secondary in the NFL. Safeties Deron Cherry and Lloyd Burruss and cornerbacks Albert Lewis and Kevin Ross made life miserable for opposing quarterbacks.

The improved Chiefs made the playoffs in 1986, losing in the first round to the New York Jets. Despite the success, Mackovic was fired. The players couldn't relate to him, Lamar Hunt said. Frank Gansz replaced Mackovic, but the Chiefs slumped again.

Outside linebacker Derrick Thomas recorded 10 quarterback sacks in his rookie season.

OKOYE IS A BIG HIT IN KANSAS CITY

In Gansz's first year, the Chiefs found a gem in the 1987 draft, a 6-foot-3, 260-pound bruiser of a runner named Christian

21

Running back Marcus Allen joined the Chiefs in the 1990s.

Okoye. Okoye grew up in Nigeria and came to the United States on a track scholarship to Azusa Pacific University in California. When he got to Azusa, Okoye noticed a strange new game called football. So he asked Azusa's track coach, Dr. Terry Franson, if he could play for Azusa's football team. "Why do you want to play?" Franson asked.

"Because," Okoye said, "I think I could be a professional player." A couple of years later, he was. The Chiefs had themselves a Nigerian fullback whom Franson called "one of the best big athletes in the world." Okoye wasn't used that much during Gansz's two years with the Chiefs. But in 1989 new coach Marty Schottenheimer decided the Chiefs had to give Okoye the ball more—a lot more. And Okoye responded by leading the NFL in rushing.

"I can remember Marty asking me, 'How many times do you think you can carry the ball in a game?'" Okoye reflected. "I told him I once carried 40 times in college. I told him I often carried 30 times a game at Azusa. Marty was surprised I told him I could do that. It is no problem for me."

Okoye impressed his offensive linemen as well as Schottenheimer. "To feel the force he runs with is amazing," said tackle Irv Eatman. "He has slammed into my back on running plays a few times, and the only way I can describe what it feels like is to imagine standing on the street and getting hit by a car going fifty miles an hour."

Marty Schottenheimer led the Chiefs to an 11-5 record his second season.

PLAYOFF STREAK IN THE NINETIES

In the 1990s, the Chiefs established themselves, under Schottenheimer's steady hand, as perennial contenders. Kansas City made it to the AFC playoffs for six straight years

24 *Left to right: Christian Okoye, Deron Cherry, Derrick Thomas, Barry Word.*

from 1990 to 1995—the longest streak by any NFL team in the decade. The Chiefs' success bore out the philosophy of their head coach. "The best way to establish a position of excellence in the NFL," Schottenheimer once explained, "is to expect it." Schottenheimer expected nothing less, and his players did not let him down.

Derrick Thomas built on his rookie achievements to have one of the greatest years ever by a defensive player in 1990. Thomas not only led the league with 20 sacks, he also set an NFL record by tallying seven sacks in a single game against the Seattle Seahawks. Veteran quarterback Steve DeBerg led the Chiefs offense, which featured Barry Word, a free agent running back, as a new threat to accompany Okoye in the backfield. The Chiefs finished 11-5, their best record since their Super Bowl season of 1969, but fell to Miami 17-16 in the first round of the playoffs.

1 9 9 3

Cornerback Albert Lewis led the Chiefs with six interceptions and bolstered their pass defense.

The following year, the Chiefs went one step better by recording their first playoff win since that Super Bowl season by defeating the Los Angeles Raiders 10-6 in a hard-fought Wild Card game. But Schottenheimer was convinced that the offense needed strengthening. For 1992, free agent Dave Krieg, a former Seattle Seahawk standout, led the Chiefs to a winning season. But in the first round of the playoffs, the Chiefs were shut down by the San Diego Chargers 17-0. Schottenheimer then decided that he would go one big step further in his search for a quarterback: he would acquire a legend.

Joe Montana had led the San Francisco 49ers to four Super Bowl victories. In three of those Super Bowls, Montana was named the Most Valuable Player—an indication of just how well "Joe Cool" could play in pressure situations. But Montana was

Derrick Thomas became the Chiefs' all-time sack leader (pages 26-27).

1 9 9 6

Defensive end Neil Smith provides veteran leadership and ignites the Chiefs' pass rush.

out for nearly all of the 1991 and 1992 seasons with an elbow injury, and the 49ers decided to make Steve Young their quarterback of the future. The Chiefs believed that Montana could regain his superstar status, and so they traded to acquire the future Hall of Famer.

Montana repaid the trust that the Chiefs had in him. In 1993, he was named AFC Offensive Player of the Week four times while leading Kansas City to an 11-5 record and its first division championship in 22 years. Montana didn't do it all alone. Just before the season started, the Chiefs also acquired free agent running back Marcus Allen, a long-time star with the Raiders who had ridden the bench in recent seasons. With Kansas City, Allen proved that his skills were still intact by rushing for 764 yards and balancing Montana's precision passing attack. The Chiefs made it all the way to the AFC championship game before falling to the Buffalo Bills 30-13.

Montana retired after the 1994 season, but Schottenheimer and the Chiefs continued their winning ways. Their new starting quarterback, Steve Bono, was Montana's former back-up at San Francisco. The Chiefs traded for Bono in the belief that he was ready to become a starter, and once again they were right. Bono ably guided the Chiefs to a 13-3 regular season record in 1995—the best in the entire NFL. Meanwhile, the defense, led by Pro Bowlers Derrick Thomas, Dale Carter, and Neil Smith, dominated opposing offenses.

Kansas City was upset in the first round of the playoffs by the "Cinderella" Indianapolis Colts, and head coach Schottenheimer faced criticism about his failure to make it to the Super Bowl. But he remained proud of his team's achievements—and of his own efforts. "I think people will look at me in 10 years and say, 'The guy is a pretty good football coach.'"

Quarterback Joe Montana.

Dominant defensive end Neil Smith was a four-time Pro Bowler.

Quarterback Steve Bono emerged as a starter in 1995.

As for the Chiefs, they have proven that they are more than a "pretty good" football team. No team has won more consistently in the 1990s than Kansas City. It may only be a matter of time before the Chiefs claim the Super Bowl crown once more. Loyal Kansas City fans deserve no less.